Gwen's Great Gizmos

Adapted by Melissa Lagonegro
from the script "Gizmo Gwen" by Michael G. Stern

Illustrated by the Disney Storybook Art Team

 A GOLDEN BOOK • NEW YORK

randomhousekids.com
ISBN 978-0-7364-3448-5 (trade) — ISBN 978-0-7364-3449-2 (ebook)
Printed in the United States of America
10 9 8 7 6 5 4 3 2 1

Princess Sofia is picking blueberries in the royal garden. She notices that her basket isn't as full as it was a minute ago.

"You can come out now, Clover. I know it's you," says Sofia with a giggle.

Clover pops out of the bushes, his mouth full of berries.

"I told Amber I would pick a basket of blueberries for the big Berry Banquet she's hosting tonight," Sofia tells her rabbit friend. "If you help, maybe you can come, too."

Before long, Sofia's basket is filled to the top!

In the castle, Sofia's sister, Amber, is busy planning her banquet. Sofia returns from the garden and shows her the basket of berries.

Amber examines a berry. "Hmm. They're not quite perfect enough for the main buffet," she says. "Everything has to be perfect for my Berry Banquet!"

"Each party guest will receive a hand-painted berry bowl that I had made especially for the banquet," declares Amber. "Then they will fill their bowls with the best berries in the kingdom."

"Speaking of berries, what should I do with these?" asks Sofia.

"Take them to the kitchen," says Amber. "Chef Andre can use them for the muffins."

Sofia enters the kitchen, and a bubbling object zooms past her.

"Look out! Runaway sponge!" yells Gwen, the kitchen maid. She chases the sponge around the kitchen. She finally traps it under a pot lid.

"I've never seen a sponge like that before," says Sofia.

"That's because I just invented it," replies Gwen. "I invent things in my spare time. I call them my gizmos."

Gwen fixes the sponge. Then Sofia watches as it cleans a dirty pot—all by itself!

Gwen's father, Chef Andre, enters the kitchen. He isn't happy with the mess Gwen's gizmo made.

"Papa doesn't like it when I make gizmos," says Gwen. "Guess I'll put this one with the others."

Gwen takes Sofia to her gizmo room and shows off her special inventions. There is a Built-in-Baker Cupcake Maker, a Teeter-Totter Rug Swatter, and even a Bicycle Built for Tunes!

"These gizmos are great!" exclaims Sofia.

Back in the ballroom, Amber directs the servants as they hang a giant strawberry from the ceiling.

"Just a bit higher . . . higher . . . ," she says.

But the giant strawberry is too heavy. The rope snaps—and the strawberry falls, crushing Amber's berry bowls!

Gwen and Sofia hear the crash and run into the ballroom.

"My berry bowls!" shouts Amber. "Without my berry bowls, my banquet won't be perfect!"

Sofia has an idea. "Gwen, do you think you can make a gizmo that paints berry bowls really fast?" she asks.

"I'll give it a go," replies Gwen.

Gwen quickly writes a list of all the things she will need to build her new gizmo.

"I hope we can get it all together in time," she says.

"Don't worry—I have some friends who can help," replies Sofia. She meets with her animal friends and sends them throughout the castle to gather supplies.

Later that day, Gwen puts the finishing touches on her new Berry Bowl Painter.

Sofia tests it out. "It's perfect! Gwen, you did it!" she exclaims.

Sofia and Gwen take the invention into the ballroom to show Amber. They don't notice that a screw has fallen out.

When Gwen turns on the machine, it starts to shake and grumble. Bowls fly all over the room, and paint sprays everywhere! The ballroom is a disaster!

"You were supposed to save my party, not wreck it!" Amber yells at Gwen.

Chef Andre enters the messy ballroom. "Gwen, please tell me that this is not one of your gizmos!"

"It is, Papa," replies Gwen with her head hung low. She knows it's time to give up her dream of being a great inventor.

Meanwhile, Whatnaught the squirrel finds a screw on the floor. He realizes it's from Gwen's Berry Bowl Painter and runs to show Sofia.

"So that's why the gizmo went haywire!" exclaims Sofia. "I've got to tell Gwen!"

Sofia finds Gwen working in the kitchen. She shows her the screw. "You can fix everything now!" says Sofia.

"No, I can't, Sofia," says Gwen sadly. "I'm no inventor."

But Sofia encourages Gwen to believe in herself and follow her dreams.

Gwen fixes her Berry Bowl Painter and takes it back into the ballroom.

Just then, Chef Andre arrives. "Gwen, what are you doing?" he cries.

"It's my dream, Papa. I have to try," Gwen replies, and she turns on the machine.

The machine clangs and bangs, and then the bowls begin to move along the conveyor belt. The paint sprays them perfectly. Gwen's invention works!

"It's beautiful!" says Amber.

"Gwen, you are an inventor—a real inventor!" exclaims Chef Andre.

Gwen beams with pride!

But Amber still isn't happy. "This room is a mess," she complains. "The cake is ruined, and the instruments are covered in paint. There's no time to fix everything!"

Sofia has an idea! They can use Gwen's other gizmos to clean up the mess, make cupcakes, and play music.

Thanks to Gwen's gizmos, the Berry Banquet is back on!

King Roland is impressed with all of Gwen's wonderful inventions.

"If it weren't for her, there wouldn't be a Berry Banquet!" Amber tells her father.

"In recognition of her outstanding inventions, I hereby appoint Gwen Enchancia's royal inventor!" the king declares.

Gwen is elated!

"Thank you, Sofia," says Gwen. "None of this would have happened without your help!"

"And me!" says Amber, smiling. "Don't forget me!"